Wind Bird

Gift of the Mist

Wind Bird

Written by
Sarah Stiles Bright

Illustrated by
Gustav Moore

Gift of the Mist

Maine Lakes Conservancy Institute, Nobleboro, Maine

ISBN-13: 978-0-9778703-0-1
ISBN-10: 0-9778703-0-8
Library of Congress Control Number: 2006924462

Designed and composed in Brioso Pro at Hobblebush Books,
Brookline, New Hampshire (www.hobblebush.com)

Printed in the United States of America

Published by:

THE MAINE LAKES CONSERVANCY INSTITUTE (MLCI) is an environmental education organization dedicated to understanding, preserving, and sustaining the health and values of Maine's lakes and the communities dependent upon them. Since its inception in 1999, MLCI has developed hands-on educational programs focused on Maine's lake resources: our Lake Science Education Program for middle school children and our highly acclaimed, interactive, and informative Civic Program. These programs teach participants to better understand how lakes work and how a lake's health directly affects our environment, our economy, and our communities.

Our Lake Science Education Program has been recognized by National Project WET (Water Education for Teachers) with its Outstanding Contributor Award in 2001, the Environmental Protection Agency with its 2002 Environmental Merit Award, and the North American Lake Management Society with its 2003 award for Public Education and Outreach. In 2004, MLCI was featured by The George Lucas Education Foundation as an "unsung hero of American education" for our web-based Student's Portal, a component of our multidisciplinary project-based education program.

P.O. BOX 55 • NOBLEBORO, MAINE 04555 • 207-563-6529 • WWW.MLCI.ORG

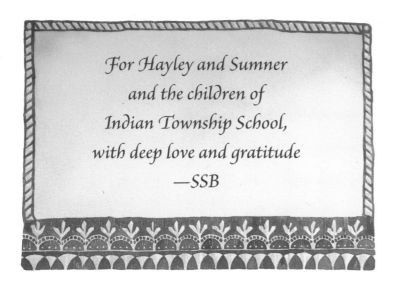

For Hayley and Sumner
and the children of
Indian Township School,
with deep love and gratitude
—SSB

Acknowledgments

THIS BOOK is indebted to the ancestors of the Passamaquoddy Tribe and we hope it will inspire others to take to heart the ancient wisdom of a people who learned to live life in balance with the earth.

The Wind Bird story is told in many variations and it is this fluid oral history that allows us to pass down wisdom from one generation to another in a way that makes sense to the present generation.

This book has been made possible by a generous grant from the Otto Fund, and gives the Passamaquoddy Tribe and the Maine Lakes Conservancy Institute the opportunity to inspire present and future generations to be responsible stewards of our freshwater natural resources for the collective benefit of all life.

We hope that this book will become part of your family's permanent collection, to pass down to future generations— and to pass on what The Ancients learned and wanted us to know.

Wayne Newell,
Tribal and Cultural leader,
Indian Township Passamaquoddy Tribe

Shippen Bright,
Executive Director and Founder,
Maine Lakes Conservancy Institute

Have you ever sat by the edge of a lake and watched the wind crawl across the water, leapfrogging in tiny, dark ripples? Have you listened to it scream on stormy days from one end of the lake toward the other, blowing the water in tight, wild whitecapped waves? Perhaps you've wondered about the creatures that live and move silently along the shore or beneath the waters, or maybe you have wondered about all that came there before you and all that will come after. I have. And when I do, I am reminded of an old story about a lake and its people—a story that was told to me by a friend and great Passamaquoddy storyteller whose people know their lake better than anyone else because they have lived there for thousands of years. He tells me that the beautiful mist over the lake in the mornings and the evenings is actually a gift given to his people by Wocawson, the Wind Bird. This is the story of that gift.

Long, long ago, in a land of the North Country, an ancient people lived between dark evergreen-forested hills and the deep, clear waters of a beautiful lake. The people farmed the land and harvested the crops. They fished the lake and brought home baskets filled with perch, bass, and trout. And they hunted the woods and brought home meat and skins to feed and clothe their families.

Life was rich with great bounties from the Water and the Earth, and the people were grateful to their hero, Gluskop, the first Man of their people, the one who came before all others in the dawn of their time. He was their caretaker and had great powers, and the people believed it was he who helped provide the land's riches for them. They fished and hunted tirelessly and celebrated their good fortune and their bounteous life.

There came a time when the wind began to blow very hard across the lake. It blew down from the nearby mountains and bent the trees so far over that many of them snapped and fell to the ground. It blew through the people's village and destroyed some of their homes. It shrieked across the lake and made the waters so rough their boats were blown far up onto the land. The wind blew so hard that the people could not fish and they could not hunt. They could not grow anything because the wind ripped the crops right out of the earth. The wind was vicious and it blew every day, and the people grew hungry.

Wocawson

~

WO-JOW-SON

~

Wind

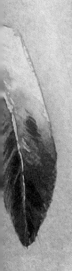

The people of the village came together one day to talk about what they could do. They sent the strongest men out to the lake to bring in their catches, but when the men went to their fishing weirs they discovered there were no fish in them. And when they went to the fields to harvest the crops they found the plants were broken and lay strewn all about the ground. And when they went to the woods to hunt for meat and bring back furs and skins, the forests were littered with broken trees and there were no animals, not even their tracks, in sight.

The people of the village were desperate. So it was decided that some of the people's leaders would travel to the woods beyond the village to find their hero, Gluskop, who was powerful and strong and could make great things happen. When they found him in his place, they spoke of their trouble, of their thirsting people and their starving children. They asked him if there was something he could do to help ease their hardship. Gluskop listened with a great caring heart, for he loved his people well. Gluskop said he would visit Grandfather Wind Bird, who, with his gigantic, powerful wings, made the wind blow. Gluskop would go to the great bird, and tell him of the people's suffering, and he would ask the Wind Bird to make the wind less fierce.

Gluskop

~

GA-LOOS-GOB

~

Gluskop

The Wind Bird lived in a faraway place, high in the mountains of the North Country. It was a difficult journey for Gluskop to make even with his great strength and endurance. The mountain peak was tall and the path to where the Wind Bird lived was very steep and treacherous. Gluskop grew weary with every step.

When Gluskop arrived at the place where the Wind Bird lived, the giant bird was sitting upon a large boulder flapping his huge, magnificent wings. The wind swirled in great twisted gusts and roared from underneath the bird's feathery arms, and when Gluskop spoke he had to raise his voice above the loudness of the wind.

"Wind Bird!" he called in his booming voice.

The Wind Bird did not answer.

Gluskop called out again, "Wind Bird! It is I, Gluskop."

But the giant bird's wings did not slow. They beat harder, and the sound from underneath them pounded like a giant drumbeat. The Wind Bird glared at Gluskop with his great round eyes and then slowly he bellowed, "Why have you come?"

"The people have asked that I speak with you. The wind you make with your wings is too great," Gluskop bellowed back. "The people are suffering. They cannot go out in their boats to fish. The trees of the forest are falling to the ground as if they were twigs, and the people cannot hunt. Their crops are torn from the ground, and they have nothing to harvest. The wind you make is too strong."

Uwon

~

OO-IN

~

Mist

When he heard this, the Wind Bird grew angry. He raised himself up and stood tall upon the boulder, and stretching his wings wide he roared, "I was here long before any man or woman could speak, long before they walked the Earth, before they hunted, before they fished these waters. I was here when the rivers and the lakes were filled to their edges with fish, and my kind always had plenty of fish to feed their young. The waters were clean and no man or woman disturbed the peace of these places where your kind now dwell. No messenger will tell me what to do with my wings!" With that, the Wind Bird drew back his head and began to beat his wings even harder. The air gushed and swirled in violent waves around the mountaintop.

The force of the wind was so great that Gluskop could not stand up for fear of being blown from the top of the mountain. But when he heard the Wind Bird declare himself he, too, grew angry and so Gluskop bravely stood up and became taller than the Wind Bird. He said to the Wind Bird as he looked down at him, "I, too, am strong. Stronger even than you! My people cannot endure the harshness of your wings any longer. If you will not calm the wind, then I will have to tie your wings down."

And this is what Gluskop did. Lunging forward before he was blown from the mountaintop, he wrestled with the giant bird. He grabbed the great wings and with strong pieces of leather tied the Wind Bird's wings back so the bird could not move them at all. To be sure that his people would be safe, Gluskop found two giant rocks near the peak of the bird's mountain and he placed the Wind Bird between those boulders where he could not free himself. All around the mountaintop, the air grew still and very quiet; the roar of the great wind was gone. Gluskop looked down upon the valley and the lake below, and he was pleased to think how happy his people would be to find that the fierce wind had finally stopped.

When Gluskop returned to the village the people were fishing again in their boats. The days were sunny and warm, and the men and women and children could enjoy being on the waters of their lake. They could go into the woods and hunt, and they could work in their fields harvesting their crops. The people were happy again.

Qospem

~

GWIS-SPAM

~

Lake

But their happiness did not last. Without the cooling movement of the wind, the lake became sick. The water did not move gently from one shore to another and from the surface to the silty bottom; the lake could not breathe the way a lake needs to breathe when its waters move back and forth, up and down. Instead the lake smelled of decaying plants and fish that died in the water, which had become thick with weeds. The people could not work in the fields for the air was too still and the sun beat down hard and there was no relief from the heat. Their crops were drying up, and the animals of the forest had moved away to find water. Again, the people were suffering.

So again, the people called on Gluskop to help them, and again Gluskop went to the mountain peak where the Wind Bird lived. The great bird was just where Gluskop had left him many weeks earlier.

"Wind Bird," said Gluskop to the bird, who was crouched between the boulders looking very sad and lonely. "My people once more are suffering. The air does not move at all. The wind does not bring the rains from far-off places. The lake is growing sicker every day, and the fish are dying. There is little food for the people to eat and no water for them to drink."

"You were wrong to tie my wings back," said the Wind Bird wearily but with some strange satisfaction in his voice.

"We were both wrong, Wind Bird," answered Gluskop, also in a weary voice. He went on wisely, "I was wrong to tie *both* your wings back. You were wrong to be so arrogant and think only of yourself and your kind. Such selfishness will only bring harm to the Earth and all its living things. You will grow old and be alone in the world. Together we must make this right."

The Wind Bird grew silent, for he knew that Gluskop was right. Gluskop helped him out of the space between the boulders and untied the leather straps that bound one of his wings in place. The Wind Bird moved the free wing, stretching it and its beautiful feathers wide. Soon a gentle breeze swirled around the mountaintop like ribbon.

"This is a good wind," said Gluskop to the Wind Bird.

Wind Bird nodded. The two were quiet, and they sat together atop the mountain looking out over the vast valley below, each thinking how beautiful a place it was with its deep green forests and the glassy lake staring back at the blue sky like the giant eye of the land's soul.

"I will agree to use only one of my wings to make the wind over the lake," the Wind Bird said, breaking the silence. "It will be a good wind for the people." This pleased Gluskop greatly. The Wind Bird went on, "But you will tell the people that they must take only what they can use from the water and the woods and the fields. If they take too much I will again see that they cannot hunt or fish or farm."

Gluskop agreed and was happy with the Wind Bird's decision. He knew that they must all share the work of keeping the lake good for fishing, the woods good for hunting, and the fields good for growing crops. "I will tell my people. If the wind begins to blow hard I will know—and the people will know—that you are angry again. And the people will learn to use only what they need from the water and the land."

Gluskop sat proudly with the Wind Bird on his mountaintop for a long time. Finally he spoke. "Wind Bird, we must give the people something so that many years from now, when different generations of my people live along these shores, they will remember the importance of the wind. They will know always to respect the gifts of the land and the water."

The Wind Bird stood high on his boulder on the top of the mountain. One more time he stretched his feathered wings wide and he tipped his head up toward the sky. He breathed in, and after filling his great chest, he let out a giant breath. The Wind Bird beat his wings in great gentle arcs and sent his breath down the side of his mountain perch. The great bird's warm breath spread across the valley below and then across the lake, where it settled in a soft mist upon the waters of the people's lake.

Kulankey-utomonen

~

GOO-LUN-KAY-
OO-ED-DA-MA-NEN

~

Let us care for it together.

Then the Wind Bird spoke:

"Your people will see the mist over their waters in the stillness of the morning and in the evening. From one generation to the next they will remember the lessons of their ancestors and they will know what it is to love the land and the water of their place."

Gluskop smiled and then bid farewell to his friend. It was time
to return to his people. When he arrived back at the village, the
people stood on the shore of their lake in the early evening gazing
at the beautiful mist that had settled gently over the water. Gluskop
gathered them and told them about the Wind Bird's wishes, and
when one of the men asked about the mist on the water, Gluskop
told them it was a gift for all generations. The people were in awe
and promised Gluskop to always honor the richness of their home—
by living wisely there.   ◊

The Passamaquoddies of Maine

The Passamaquoddy tribe resides in Washington County in eastern Maine. Oral tribal history and the science of archeology both indicate that the Passamaquoddies have been there for at least six thousand years. The tribal membership is currently about three thousand members. The indigenous language of the tribe is still spoken. The land base of the tribe is about three hundred thousand acres in various parts of Washington County and in western Maine. The tribe is self-governing but shares some common governmental authority with the state of Maine, such as fishing on lakes within its territory. The Passamaquoddy Tribe strives to use its natural resources according to traditional values long held by our ancestors.

-Wayne Newell, *Tribal and Cultural leader, Indian Township Passamaquoddy Tribe*